THE MAGIC WHEEL

WRITTEN BY BRIAN BIRCHALL
ILLUSTRATED BY ROB MANCINI

Columbus, OH • Chicago, IL • Redmond, WA

CONTENTS

INTRODUCTION

The world is full of wheels.
Look around—
you'll find them everywhere . . .
spinning along highways,
whirling in parks and playgrounds,
hidden away inside toys and engines.
Everywhere that people
work and play and move and carry,
there are wheels turning and turning,
doing their special work.

No one knows who made the first wheel.
That person's name and face
are lost in the long, long ago.
But that invention has changed people's lives
more than any other.

No longer are we slow, shuffling earth creatures,
plodding over the ground on tired feet.

With the spinning magic of wheels,
we can speed along faster than a cheetah . . .
soar higher than an eagle . . .
hover like a bumblebee . . .
lift heavy loads as easily as an elephant.

We have become super creatures,
with incredible powers —
all because of the magic wheel.

WHEELS FOR CARRYING

You have a big box to carry home,
and your little brother is tired.

You carry the box under one arm
and your little brother under the other.

Then you carry the box in front of you,
and your brother rides on your back.

The box and the brother seem to get heavier
and heavier, as you walk along.

Along comes a friend, pulling a wagon.
In goes the heavy box.
In goes the heavy brother.
Now, moving that load is so much easier.
The wagon wheels are carrying the weight.
All you have to do is pull the load along.

With wheels, it is easy to move a heavy load.
Suddenly, you feel as strong as an elephant!

HOW THEY WORK

The wheels on a wagon work like this:

A bar, called an axle,
is fixed to the bottom of a box.

The wagon wheels have a hole
in the center, to fit the axle.

As long as the wheels can spin freely
on the axle, the wagon is easy
to pull along.

SOMETHING TO TRY

Rollers and wheels can be used
to help move heavy weights.

Put a piece of a wooden pole or a steel pipe
under a heavy box.
This works as a roller.
When you push the box,
see how easily it moves along.

WHEELS FOR SPEEDING

When you ride a bicycle,
you can travel along swiftly and smoothly—
faster than you can walk,
and faster than you can run.

Riding a bicycle, you can travel farther in one day—
farther than you can walk,
and farther than you can run.

As you ride swiftly along on your bicycle,
as you feel the wind in your face,
as you see the ground flashing along under you,
you ride a magic set of wheels.

HOW THEY WORK

The wheels on a bicycle work like this:

The pedals on your bicycle
are fastened to a sprocket wheel.

When you push the pedals around,
the sprocket wheel turns,
and the chain carries your leg power
to drive the back wheel
that sends you speeding along.

Sprocket wheels and chains work like this:

A sprocket wheel has pointed teeth
around its outside edge.

The teeth fit into the holes in a chain.
This stops the chain from slipping.

Now the chain can carry power
from one sprocket wheel to another.

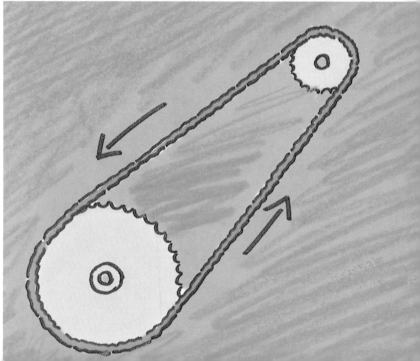

SOMETHING TO TRY

Turn the bicycle upside down.
Turn the pedals around with your hand.
See how much faster the back wheel turns
than the pedals do.

Make a mark on the back wheel,
then turn the pedal around once.

Count how many times the big wheel goes around
for one full turn of the pedal.

*But keep your fingers away from the sprockets
and the chain.*

12

WHEELS FOR GLIDING AND WHEELS FOR LIFTING

Go for a ride on a sit-harness.
Feel how you glide along through the air.
Feel how you glide along, so quickly and smoothly.

If you were to run down the same hill, you would be
kicking up stones,
stepping in holes,
pushing through the bushes.

But, riding on the sit-harness,
you swoop down the hill like a bird.

When you ride on a sit-harness,
listen to the wheel humming,
as it glides smoothly along the rope.
The wheel lets you fly like a bird.
The secret of the sit-harness lies in its special wheel.

HOW THEY WORK

A sit-harness works like this:

The sit-harness has a wheel
that lets you travel along the rope.

The wheel has a groove around its outside edge.
The groove keeps the wheel running along the rope.

A wheel like this is called a pulley.

You want to fly a flag from the top of a flagpole.
It's a long way up the pole.
It's a long, hard climb all the way up to the top,
with a flag in your hand.

But you can hoist the flag to the top of the pole
without climbing up and down.

You can do it if you have a pulley
at the top of the pole,
and enough rope to reach
from the bottom of the pole to the top
and back down again.

SOMETHING TO TRY

You can fly a flag like this:

Tie the top of the flag
to one end of the rope.

Tie the bottom of the flag
to the other end of the rope.

When you pull on one part of the rope,
the flag goes up.

When you pull on the other part of the rope,
the flag comes down.

SOMETHING TO DO

Look for pulleys where people or things
need to be moved along, or up, or down . . .

on cranes,
on venetian blinds,
on elevators,
on mountains,
on flagpoles.

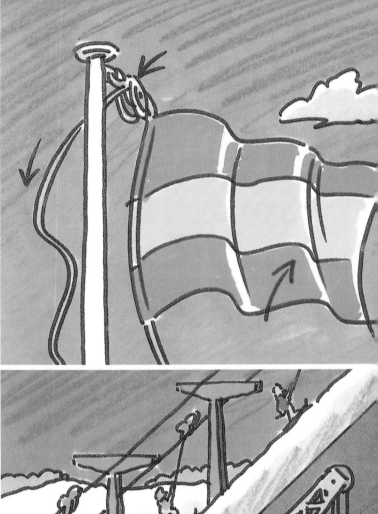

WHEELS FOR SAILING

Bikes and trucks and wagons and cars
all have wheels made for moving over land.

But some wheels are made
for moving things through water.

Some of these wheels are easy to see.

A paddle boat has two big wheels at the back.
The rider pushes the pedals,
and the pedals drive the wheels.
The paddle boat splatter-splatters along,
like a big, angry water beetle.

This steamboat has one big wheel
on each side. The big wheels turn
and pull the ship along.

Sometimes, the wheel that moves a ship
is not easy to see.

If you stand near the back of a ship
as it sails along
you will feel a rumbling and a shaking
under your feet.

Look behind, and you will see water,
all mixed and beaten up,
stretching out behind the ship.

The rumbling and the mixing and the beating
come from a big driving wheel,
working under the ship.

The ship is being pushed along
by a wheel called a propeller.

Ships and steamboats and paddle boats
all have wheels specially made
for pushing through water.

These wheels all have paddles, or blades.

The paddles on the paddle boat
and the steamboat are flat.
They are made for pulling.

They pull and pull through the water,
like the arms of a swimmer
doing the butterfly stroke.

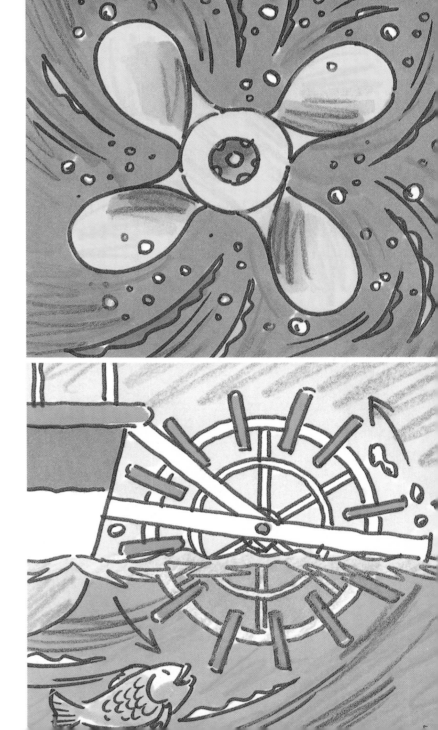

HOW THEY WORK

The blades on a ship's propeller
are not flat, but twisted.

The twisted blades push and push
against the water,
and drive the ship along.

A propeller wheel works like this:

Look at an electric fan.
See how the blades are twisted to push
against the air.

Now, switch on the fan.
Feel how the fan pushes a stream
of air into your face.

This is how the twisted blades work
on a ship's propeller,
pushing against the water,
and driving the ship along.

WHEELS FOR HOVERING AND WHEELS FOR FLYING

Perhaps you have seen a helicopter taking off . . .

Flack-flack-flack-flack!
Flack-flack-flack-flack!

The great blades on top of the helicopter whirl around, faster and faster, and then they tilt.

The helicopter lifts off the ground, and hovers in the air, like an enormous bee.

The helicopter can go up and down and hover and fly because it has wheels.

21

HOW THEY WORK

The wheels on a helicopter work like this:

The wheel on top of the helicopter has great blades fixed to the axle. These great blades are called rotors. They can tilt, to make the helicopter go up, down, and forward.

The helicopter has a smaller wheel, or propeller, at the back. This propeller steers, or directs the helicopter to the left and right.

22

Hovercraft and small airplanes also use rotors and propellers to move through the air.

SOMETHING TO DO

Look for airplanes and hovercraft. See how they use wheels and blades for hovering and for flying.

23

WHEELS FOR THRILLS

When you go to the park,
find a merry-go-round and give it a whirl.

The merry-go-round is a big wheel—
a wheel on its side,
fastened to the ground.

When you ride on the merry-go-round,
you see the park and the people
and the whole world whirling around.

The merry-go-round is a wheel
made for thrills.

24

Skateboards and roller skates are more wheels
for children to play on . . .

rolling and roaring,
flipping and turning,
riding on wheels for fun and thrills.

When people go out to play,
the wheels whirl and spin
and sing and hum.

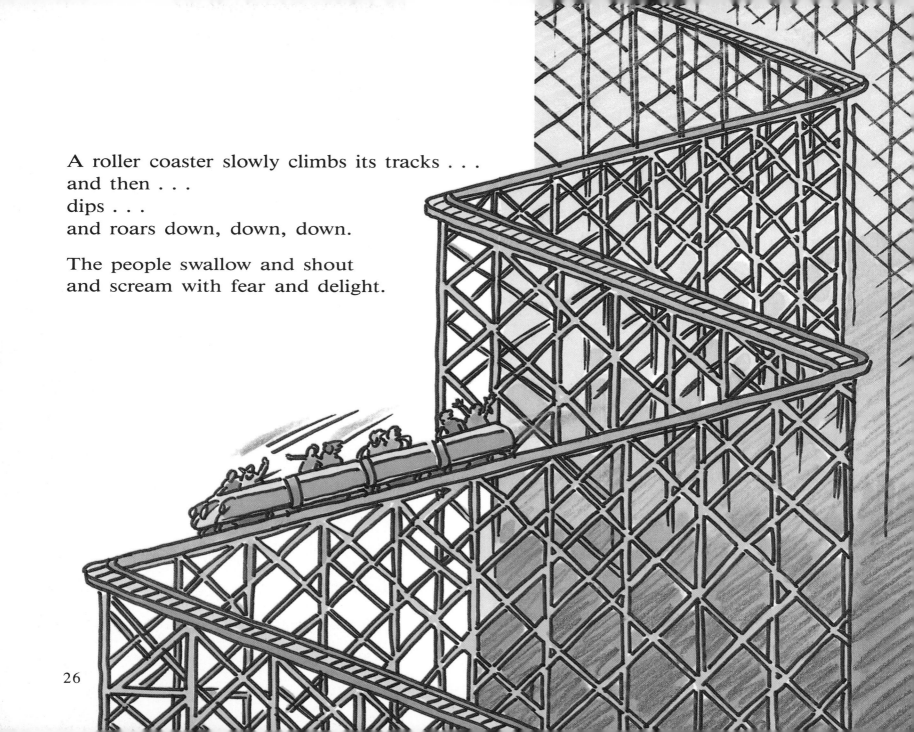

A roller coaster slowly climbs its tracks . . .
and then . . .
dips . . .
and roars down, down, down.

The people swallow and shout
and scream with fear and delight.

On the ferris wheel,
the riders swing in their seats,
high above the world.

As the great wheel turns,
the riders look down and call out
to the tiny insect people below.

And go-cart racers go pop-popping
and screeching and skidding
around their tracks.

Dirtbike riders make their machines
snarl and scream,
up hills and down dips.

Racing cars roar and screech
around their tracks
on smoking wheels.

When people are at play,
the whole world seems to be out on wheels—
wheels for thrills.

A WORLD WITHOUT WHEELS

Today, it is hard to think
how our world would be without wheels.
They are everywhere.

If creatures came to Earth from another planet —
a planet without wheels —
they would be amazed
at what they saw.

They would go home and tell
of the new planet
they had discovered —

The Planet of the Wheel People.

INDEX

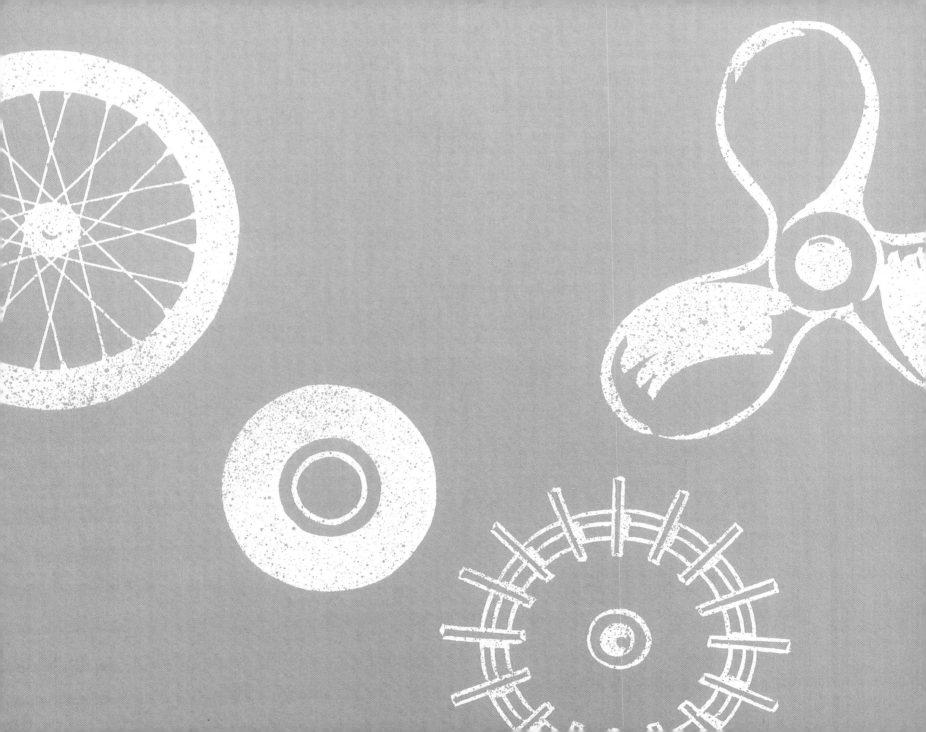